GLEN ROCK PUBLIC LIBRARY
315 ROCK ROAD
GLEN ROCK, N.J. 07452

NATIVE ❖ LATIN ❖ AMERICAN ❖ CULTURES

Eileen Lucas

Series Editor
Robert Pickering, Ph.D.

ROURKE PUBLICATIONS, INC.
Vero Beach, Florida 32964

©1995 by Rourke Publications, Inc.

All rights reserved. No part of this book may be reproduced or utilized in any form or by any means, electronic or mechanical including photocopying, recording, or by any information storage and retrieval system without permission in writing from the publisher.

Printed in the United States of America.

A Blackbirch Graphics book.

Senior Editor: Tanya Lee Stone
Assistant Editor: Elizabeth Taylor
Design Director: Sonja Kalter

Library of Congress Cataloging-in-Publication Data

Lucas, Eileen.
Trade / by Eileen Lucas.
   p. cm. — (Native Latin American cultures)
  Includes bibliographical references.
  ISBN 0-86625-555-9
    1. Indians—Commerce—Latin America—Juvenile literature.
[1. Indians—Commerce—Latin America.] I. Title. II. Series.
E59.C59L83   1995
380. 1'098 0902—dc20   95-7292
                                                                                 CIP
                                                                                   AC

Contents

		Introduction	*4*
Chapter 1	❖	Northwestern Mexico	*7*
Chapter 2	❖	The Central Valley and the Gulf Coast of Mexico	*13*
Chapter 3	❖	Southwestern Mexico, the Yucatán Peninsula, and Northern Central America	*27*
Chapter 4	❖	The Caribbean	*35*
Chapter 5	❖	The Amazon Basin	*45*
Chapter 6	❖	The Andes	*53*
		Glossary	*59*
		Further Reading	*61*
		Index	*62*

Introduction

The towering temples and fierce warriors of the Aztecs, the sophisticated lords of the Maya, and the vast empire of the Inca that extended along the Andes are all images that come to mind when the native cultures of Mexico, Central America, and South America are mentioned. While these images are real, they are only a small part of the story of the indigenous peoples of the Americas. More important, there are hundreds of other cultures that are not as well known, but just as interesting. To explore the cultures of this huge area is to examine the great diversity and richness of humanity in the Americas.

This series on *Native Latin American Cultures* presents six books, each with a major theme: the arts, daily customs, spirituality, trade, tribal rules, and the invasion by Europeans. It focuses mainly on pre-Columbian times (before the arrival of Columbus in the New World) through about 1800. These books illustrate the ingenuity, resourcefulness, and unique characters of many cultures. While a variety of tribes share similarities, many are extremely different from one another.

It is important to remember that the Americas were home to people long before Europeans arrived. Archaeologists have uncovered sites as old as 12,000 years. Over the years, human cultures in every part of the Americas developed and evolved. Some native cultures died out, other peoples survived as hunter-gatherers, and still others grew to create huge empires. Many native languages were not recorded and, in some instances, they have been forgotten.

But other groups, such as the Maya, did record their languages. Scientists are just now learning to read the Mayan language. Mayan stories tell of the power and glory of great rulers, heroic battles between city-states, and other important events. Massive stone temples and ruins of cities have survived from several cultures, giving us insight into the past.

Many native cultures of the Americas exist today. Some have blended with the modern cultures of their countries while maintaining their traditional ways. Other, more remote groups exist much as they did several hundred years ago. The books in the *Native Latin American Cultures* series capture the richness of indigenous cultures of the Americas, bringing past cultures alive and exploring those that have survived.

Robert Pickering, Ph.D.
Department of Anthropology
Denver Museum of Natural History

Chapter

1

Northwestern Mexico

The story of the development of trade among the native peoples of Mexico and Central and South America is the story of contact between people. Trade—the exchange of products, information, or services—requires something to exchange and someone to exchange it with. Trade may signify the first moment of foreign contact, or the beginning of a long-term relationship between different people and cultures.

The First Americans

The earliest residents of northwestern Mexico were probably the descendants of nomadic hunters who followed large animals over the Bering Strait from Asia into North America at least 10,000 years ago. They traveled from the northwest tip of North America, moving slowly southward across the vast landmass. Over many centuries, these ancient people evolved into many different groups that spoke different languages and developed in unique ways. Eventually, a number of these groups reached what is now the southwestern part of the United States and northwestern Mexico.

*Opposite:
Spanish missionaries and settlers came to northwestern Mexico for many different reasons. In Copper Canyon, Satevo church was built for both miners and natives.*

Some of them continued to push southward into Central and South America, while others stayed behind.

The ways in which these early peoples built their homes and the kinds of food they ate depended upon the resources available in their territory. For instance, people collected special kinds of flint to make tools. They also developed rules for behavior and procedures for dealing with one another and with their neighbors.

There likely was little organized trade. These nomadic hunters worked full time at finding food and shelter. They probably discovered that by sharing the results of their efforts, they could get what they needed in a more efficient way. This sharing might have led to specialization, in which some people did certain jobs (such as hunting) while others worked at other tasks (such as preparing hides for clothing). This tendency to specialize developed at different rates and in different ways in various geographic regions.

The Development of Agriculture and Trade

About 7,000 or 8,000 years ago, the wandering hunters of northern Mexico began experimenting with plant seeds. Collecting seeds was followed by planting them in ground that had been overturned with digging sticks. The first farmers probably did not stay to tend their crops, but continued instead in their nomadic rounds. It is likely, however, that they checked on their gardens and returned to harvest them. They gradually learned that the seeds of one wild plant called maize, or corn, could be planted to produce more maize. By carefully tending the crop, they could, in time, have a dependable source of food.

The invention of agriculture was an important first step in the development of complex civilization. Eventually, people spent more time settled in one place. This gave them a reason to build permanent houses and to acquire more belongings. They lived closer together and in larger groups. Tribes developed from these groups.

These major changes in lifestyle encouraged the development of a system for exchange. A more dependable supply of food resulted from agriculture, which gave people something to trade—their surplus food. In addition, it gave some of them more time to create other products to trade. Trading also created alliances between people.

The Tribes of Northwestern Mexico

The peoples who settled in northwestern Mexico had a way of life that made good use of the local plants and animals. They were the first to learn how to cultivate the small, grassy maize plant, as well as beans and squash. Gourds were raised for seeds and to make containers. They also ate those animals that they could kill, such as deer and rabbits, and gathered wild roots and berries. As a result, they were able to survive and become established in the area.

In time, separate groups with distinct cultural characteristics evolved. These included the ancestors of the Seri, the Pima, the Yaqui, the Maya, and the Opata. Some of these tribes, notably the Seri, remained semi-nomadic, moving around in their territories and relying on hunting and gathering wild food. Others, particularly the Pima, became very successful farmers. Although maize was their principal crop, they also learned to grow squash, peppers, beans, and cotton, from which they extracted fibers for weaving. The Seri, who did

The Pima built villages and established farms in the desert lowlands of northwestern Mexico.

At least 1,000 years ago, ancient northwest Mexicans mined obsidian (above) and other minerals and traded them to many parts of Mexico. The pocket knife shows the relative size of the obsidian.

little farming, sometimes traded animal hides and salt, which they collected from the sea, for food that was grown by other tribes. They also raided neighboring groups for things they wanted.

Some of the natives of northwestern Mexico were able to utilize minerals found in the hills and mountainsides of the region. They used copper to make tools and jewelry, household tools, and ceremonial objects. Some groups traded raw copper and copper items with natives to the north, in what is now California and New Mexico. In exchange for their copper, they received turquoise, which they valued for ceremonial items and jewelry. In the warm, well-watered areas of western Jalisco, natives mined and traded obsidian with the people of the central valley. Trade with tribes to the south brought them parrots and parrot feathers. From the peoples of the Pacific coast, they had seashells, with which they made ornaments and jewelry. These goods were carried over long distances by members of all tribes, either individually or in small groups. Bits of pottery have been found in the remains of villages many miles from where the pots were made, and shells have been discovered hundreds of miles from the sea. Buffalo robes made by natives of the Great Plains of North America were taken to the far-distant tribal villages of northwestern Mexico.

Trade with the Spanish

One of the first Europeans to visit northwestern Mexico was Álvar Núñez Cabeza de Vaca. Shipwrecked off the coast of Texas, Cabeza de Vaca and three companions walked across

11

Texas and Mexico in an attempt to join up with Spanish forces in Mexico City. Along the way, the four men visited many different native villages. In an Opata village, Cabeza de Vaca saw many items that this tribe had received in trade. "We continually found certain corals from the South Sea [the Pacific Ocean]," he reported later, "and fine turquoises that came from the north. To me they gave five emeralds made into arrow heads. I asked whence they got these; and they said the stones were brought from some lofty mountains that stand toward the north, where were populous towns and very large houses, and that they were purchased with plumes and the feathers of parrots."

In the hope of finding treasures like those seen in the Opata village, several Spanish expeditions set out from Mexico City in search of these "large cities" to the north. But time and time again they found the region poor in the only item they were really interested in: gold. As a result, few Spaniards initially settled in northwestern Mexico.

Eventually, however, Spanish missionaries, miners, and ranchers came to the land of the Pima and the Yaqui. Some natives moved to the missions set up by Spanish priests, where they worked as farm laborers and craftsmen. They traded the crops they grew and the crafts they made to the colonists in need of these items. Nevertheless, the Spanish found it difficult to collect in this region the tribute, or tax, that they were used to demanding from other native peoples of the New World. By Spanish standards, the natives were very poor and fiercely independent.

Over time, the number of native peoples living in northwestern Mexico was greatly reduced, owing to epidemics of disease as well as abuse by the colonists. Today, however, there are still several groups of natives in this area who cultivate corn and trade their unique crafts for goods from the modern world.

Chapter

2

The Central Valley and the Gulf Coast of Mexico

In contrast to the simple civilizations of northwestern Mexico, those of the central valley and the eastern, or Gulf, coast of Mexico gave rise to some very complex and powerful native cultures.

The Olmecs

One of the very earliest of these complex civilizations developed along the eastern coast of Mexico, in the vicinity of the present-day states of Veracruz and Tabasco. We have come to know these people, the Olmecs, by the archaeologists who have studied both the remains of their cities and the things that they made and left behind.

These archaeologists think that around the year 800 B.C., a time when most other native groups were struggling simply to survive, the Olmecs developed a rich and artistic culture. They carved marvelous stone heads, some nine feet tall.

*Opposite:
Olmec artists often carved faces into their works of art. A were-jaguar face appears on this jade ceremonial axe.*

13

14

They also made beautiful carvings in jade. Their art was in the form of pottery and statues that appear to have been more decorative than useful. They seem to have been much more culturally complex than their neighbors.

The major centers of Olmec culture, the most important cities, were along the coast on the Gulf of Mexico. Some archaeologists believe that the Olmecs visited and, perhaps, lived among other native groups in central Mexico, particularly their neighbors, the Zapotecs, in Oaxaca. It appears that the Zapotecs were not conquered by the Olmecs but, instead, were strongly influenced by them.

Like their Olmec neighbors, the Zapotec created decorative art. This sculpture shows a god emerging from a jaguar's mouth.

The Olmecs may have been one of the earliest groups in the Western Hemisphere to create organized trading relationships with other people. They were great overland travelers and made use of natural routes that followed the features of the natural terrain, such as around mountain bases and across shallow creek beds, which later cultures would also use to establish trade routes. They set up trading posts along the frequently traveled routes. Objects made by the Olmecs have been found in many distant places, including the Pacific coast of southern Mexico and Guatemala, and as far south as Honduras and Costa Rica.

In Olmec cities, craftsmen worked with the raw materials that Olmec travelers brought back from the highlands. These materials included jade and serpentine, a spotted, decorative stone. They also probably gave to the people of the highlands things that were found only in the Olmecs' hot, steamy homeland: tropical birds and their feathers, and cacao beans. They also traded objects that craftsmen had made from raw materials.

For unknown reasons, around 400 B.C. the Olmec cities began to lose their influence over their neighbors, and their trade routes became less traveled. It is not known exactly what became of the Olmec people, but it is evident that they had a tremendous effect on many other native cultures in the region. Some researchers believe that the Olmecs encouraged the development of other civilizations.

The City of Teotihuacán

Although the Olmecs were scattered (around or after 400 B.C.), people still had a need for trade. There were now many cities and groups of people competing for a role in extensive trading networks. The Totonacs, who lived in cities along the Gulf of Mexico and used canoes to travel from Veracruz southward, were one such group.

The merchants of Teotihuacán sometimes traveled far from the city to trade for raw materials needed at home. This Teotihuacán slab leg tripod pot was discovered among Mayan ruins in Tikal, Guatemala.

Soon, however, one city in particular was dominating the politics and culture. It was called Teotihuacán, and it was located farther to the west of Veracruz, in the central valley of Mexico. Some researchers describe it as "one of the really great cities of the world." It was probably the largest city in the Americas before the Spanish arrived. The native people of Teotihuacán built a huge pyramid, more than 200 feet high, known as the Pyramid of the Sun.

Teotihuacán was the home of many specialized craftsmen and the site of a great market. It was the center of a commercial and political empire, and many merchants traveled its routes. They journeyed to Oaxaca and Veracruz. They went to northern Mexico and the southwestern part of what is today the United States, carrying pottery to trade for raw materials. And they went to the south, to trade with the Maya of Kaminaljuyu.

Along the coasts of both the Gulf of Mexico and the Pacific Ocean between the city of Teotihuacán and the land of the Maya were many small cities. These became important stops along the trade routes. Each had certain natural resources or produced specialized goods that made them valuable in the trading process. Rubber for balls and feathers for headdresses were among the goods that these warm, lowland places had to offer.

The influence of the city of Teotihuacán seems to have come to an end, for largely unknown reasons, around the year A.D. 750. At this time, it seems, many of its citizens abandoned their city, perhaps because of fire or warfare.

The Toltecs, Tula, and Quetzalcoatl

After the fall of Teotihuacán, Tula was the next city to take center stage in the arena of trade. Tula was just a short distance to the north of Teotihuacán. It had previously been a small, unimportant trading partner. Tula was located near several rivers, which improved its access to other important cities in the region.

Legend has it that a great leader came to Tula, took the name of Quetzalcoatl, and led the people, known as the Toltecs, to great levels of achievement. According to this legend, "Under his leadership the arts were stimulated, and metallurgists, feather-workers, sculptors, and craftspersons of every type were assembled from other regions and encouraged

The remains of the Quetzalcoatl temple in Tula. From this city, the Toltecs traded crafts for food and luxury items.

to produce their finest work. The Toltecs excelled in all arts and sciences; hunger and misery were unknown, everything was plentiful, and all were rich and happy."

It is doubtful that conditions in Tula were quite that perfect. One part of the legend, however, was true: Many of the people of Tula were very skilled in crafts and trade. Others were important religious or administrative leaders. Because there were few farmers, though, the people of Tula had to trade the goods that they made for food, which was grown in rural areas far away from the city. Two other important imports were salt and obsidian, a volcanic glass that was used to make knife blades. Luxury items—such as cacao beans, feathers, shells, and precious stones—were also imported. The Toltecs established contact with other, distant native groups to obtain these goods.

The people of Tula spoke several different languages, and came from many different parts of Mexico. They included, perhaps, some of the refugees from Teotihuacán. This broad background may have had something to do with their willingness to do business with peoples of other cultures.

The marketplace of Tula was probably near the center of the city, and it is likely that it was near a ball court. People would have gathered on market days to exchange goods and news, and perhaps to watch a game of ball.

Around A.D. 950, the Toltecs were at the height of their influence. By A.D. 1200, however, there had been some kind of trouble in Tula. Archaeologists believe that many of the people left, and moved on to influence history in other places.

When the Toltec Empire collapsed, an opportunity for new patterns of trade and settlement to develop arose. In the central valley of Mexico, a number of small city-states and bands of semi-nomadic wanderers competed for control of resources. Eventually, new alliances were made, and it was in this environment that the Aztec Empire was born.

The Aztecs

The Aztecs (they called themselves the Mexicas) moved into the valley of Mexico around A.D. 1200. They came from the north and spoke Nahuatl, a language related to other languages in the north of Mexico.

They found the central valley already populated with many other native peoples; most of the best areas for cities and farms were already taken. The Aztecs were driven from one spot to another around the shores of a group of large, somewhat salty lakes. Eventually, they settled on a marshy island in Lake Texcoco. There they began to build the city they called Tenochtitlán, "place of the prickly pear cactus fruit." They increased the amount of land they had to work with by piling mud into little fenced-in areas in the marsh around their island. These enclosed plots of land were called *chinampas*. On these *chinampas*, the Aztecs planted maize, beans, squash, and other crops. By 1370, their island had become a town. It is estimated that soon there were some 60,000 homes in the Tenochtitlán area.

Nearby, the Aztecs built another town. This one was called Tlatelolco. In it were a magnificent temple and a large marketplace. The Aztecs built aqueducts to carry fresh water across the salty lakes to these cities. Soil-and-stone bridges, called causeways, were constructed so that the people could walk from the island cities to the mainland. Gaps in the causeways were often covered with removable platforms; these functioned like a drawbridge over a moat, protecting the cities from enemies.

Canoes were an important means of transportation both in and around Tenochtitlán, and were a convenient way to get heavy loads of material out to the city from the shore. Because of the way the *chinampas* were constructed, many sites were located on canals instead of streets. People traveled up and down these canals in canoes all the time.

In 1428, the Aztec leader Itzcoatl (his name meaning "obsidian snake") forged an alliance between Tenochtitlán, Texcoco, and Tlacopán. Together, they became known as the Triple Alliance. Under Itzcoatl's leadership, the Aztecs of Tenochtitlán conquered more of the land around them.

Generally, when the Aztecs conquered a city, they allowed their new subjects to keep their rulers and their ways of life. The main change was that those who were conquered now had to pay tribute to the Aztecs. This tribute usually took the form of foods or products. Sometimes, they had to work for the Aztecs as part of their tribute. At the peak of its power, more than 270 towns were paying tribute to the Triple Alliance, with Tenochtitlán receiving the greatest share of the riches.

Long-Distance Traders

Hand in hand with the growth of the empire came growth in trade. This growth was due in large part to the development of a class of professional traveling merchants, called *pochteca*. They traveled all over Mexico, to the outskirts of the empire and beyond. It is said that their caravans even went as far south as Panama. They could be away from Tenochtitlán for many years at a time. When they were home in the Aztec capital, they lived in their own part of the city. Only the sons of *pochteca* could become *pochteca* themselves.

The Aztecs did not have domesticated animals, such as horses or oxen, to carry loads on these long trips. Nor did they have any wheeled vehicles, such as carts, to help them with transportation. Besides using canoes, they transported goods and objects by using large numbers of human porters. This job, like the *pochteca*'s, was usually a hereditary one; and although it was not as high in status as that of the *pochteca*, it was extremely important to the Aztec way of life.

Porters played an important role in Aztec trade. They carried heavy loads of goods, using a forehead strap and a sack or basket.

Each porter carried a load of sixty to one hundred pounds. A load was usually carried in a sack or a basket on the back, held in place by a strap placed across the forehead. In this manner, the finely crafted goods of Tenochtitlán were carried to the distant corners of the Aztec Empire and beyond. Porters returned to Tenochtitlán carrying goods from the lands they had visited.

Sometimes the Aztecs established permanent trading posts in unconquered territory, such as the one in the valley of Oaxaca: Tepexi. This was an important stopping place, one that the merchants could count on for a friendly reception and a safe place to rest.

Other places visited by the *pochteca* included the west coast, where they traded for seashells, the feathers of tropical birds, and cacao, from which they made *chocolatl*, a delicious drink. They brought gold and turquoise and fine cloth mantles from Oaxaca. They brought finely carved jewelry from Veracruz, and the skins of wild animals that inhabited that eastern coast.

The most important trade route seems to have been the one that headed south, to the hot lands of the Yucatán and Guatemala. In these foreign places, the *pochteca* would trade the Aztecs' salt, obsidian, and other goods for jade, feathers, and jaguar skins.

Before a *pochteca*'s caravan left Tenochtitlán, he would make a sacrifice to the god of the merchants, Yacatecuatli. Then he would watch for a sign that it was indeed a good time to set out on a journey. The merchant would make another offering to Yacatecuatli if he returned safely.

For these traveling merchants of the Aztecs, life was filled with many dangers. Some of those were natural, such as flooded rivers and hot deserts to cross, and the possibility of hunger and thirst if supplies ran out. The others were man-made; there was always the chance of being attacked by enemies of the Aztecs.

When traveling through unconquered territory, the *pochteca* often acted as spies. Upon their return to the city of Tenochtitlán, they would report to the king all that they had learned of the strengths and weaknesses of their clients. They would advise the Aztec king on the probability of conquering those people. There were even some cases of *pochteca* themselves taking a territory for the empire! Even if the *pochteca* did not usually fight, the information they provided was extremely valuable.

Marvelous Marketplaces

The *pochteca* were the long-distance merchants, but there were local sellers of goods as well. Food and household items needed by the citizens of Tenochtitlán and other Aztec cities were traded in local marketplaces. Peasants walked and canoed to these markets from all over the countryside. As the center of the Aztec world, the marketplace of Tenochtitlán was quite spectacular. When the Spanish conquistador (conqueror) Hernando Cortés first saw it, he described it for his king with these words:

"The city has many squares where they are always holding markets, and carrying on trade. One of these squares is twice as large as that of Salamanca [a city in Spain], and is surrounded by arcades where there are daily more than sixty thousand souls buying and selling, and where are found all the kinds of commodities produced in these lands, including foodstuffs, jewels of gold and silver, lead, brass, copper, tin, stone, bones, shells and feathers....There is a street for game where they sell all kinds of birds, such as chickens, partridges, quails, wild ducks, turtledoves, pigeons, parrots, owls, eaglets, falcons. They also sell rabbits, hares, venison, and small dogs.

"There is a street set apart for the sale of herbs. There are houses where they sell medicines in the form of liquids, ointments, and plasters. There are places like our barber shops where they wash and shave their heads. There are all sorts of vegetables, especially onions, leeks, watercress and artichokes. There are many kinds of fruits, among others, cherries and plums. They sell bees' honey and wax, and honey made from maize stalks, which is as sweet and syrupy as that of sugar.

"They also sell skeins of different kinds of cotton, in all colors. They also sell as many painter's colors as in Spain and tanned deerskin, both white and of different colors, and much earthen ware, most of it glazed and painted.

"They sell maize, both in the kernel and made into bread. They sell bird pies and fish pastries, eggs of hen and geese, and tortillas made of eggs.

"Each kind of merchandise is sold in its proper street, and they do not mix their merchandise. Everything is sold to count and measure."

The busy marketplace at Tenochtitlán, as captured in a large mural by Mexican artist Diego Rivera. Here, household items are being traded.

What Cortés meant by "everything is sold to count and measure" is that the Aztecs had figured out a way to set a value on various items. For example, a certain amount of maize had a certain value, and a certain size of pot had a certain value. Therefore, a gourdful of maize, for example, might be exchanged for a pot that the maize grower needed. The person who had accepted the maize as payment for the pot might later exchange it for some tortillas and beans. Cacao beans, copper blades, and gold dust were commodities that were repeatedly exchanged, becoming almost like money.

There was an overseer, or person in charge of the market, and many rules were set down regarding the proper way to trade. It was against the law to trade goods on the way to the market, as this might offend the god of the market. Someone accused of stealing in the marketplace was likely to be beaten on the spot. The overseer and his many assistants made sure that goods being traded were of acceptable quality and that prices were fair.

End of an Empire

In 1519, Hernando Cortés landed on the coast of Mexico near Veracruz. There he encountered the Totonac, who had recently been conquered by the Aztecs. They told Cortés that the Aztecs had an enormous amount of gold. In an effort to escape from the tribute that they were forced to pay the Aztecs, and because they knew that they could not defeat the Spanish, the Totonac agreed to help Cortés conquer the Aztecs. With the help of these and other native allies, Cortés succeeded in destroying Tenochtitlán and ending the reign of the Aztec kings over Mexico.

From the rubble of Tenochtitlán, the Spanish conquistadores built their own city. They renamed it Mexico City. Soon they controlled all of Mexico, including land to the north and south of it. This huge colony was called New Spain. Virtually all economic traffic in New Spain was directed through Mexico City.

Cortés and other Spaniards sent ships from the western coast of Mexico to the Moluccas—islands in the Malay Archipelago—and to Manila, in the Philippines. The silver and gold of Mexico was used by the Europeans to buy exotic Asian goods such as silks, spices, rare woods, jade, and ivory.

The Spanish relied at first on the trade and communication routes established by the native people to run Mexico as a Spanish colony. Later, they built roads that suited their purposes of consolidating control of Mexico and spreading their culture throughout the colony.

In the seventeenth century, as Spanish colonists settled down to life in New Spain, they often lived on haciendas, Spanish-owned farms or ranches. The natives lived in small, poor communities called reductions. The Spanish introduced a number of things that are still found in Mexico today. These include sombreros, horses, sheep, cattle, and donkeys.

Although the great cultures of Teotihuacán, Tula, and Tenochtitlán have disappeared, the people of Mexico still trade in colorful, lively marketplaces. In Mexico City and many other places, sturdy woven baskets, beautifully crafted jewelry, and exotic fruits and vegetables are still exchanged for the currency of the day.

Chapter

3

Southwestern Mexico, the Yucatán Peninsula, and Northern Central America

Opposite: Mayan cities, such as Tikal, located in Petén, Guatemala, included temples, living areas, and markets.

Several thousand years ago, there were people living in the cool highlands and the steamy lowland jungles in what are today known as the southern part of Mexico and northern Guatemala. The natives of the regions were maize farmers, whose lives were ruled by the rhythms of nature. They had contact with tribes in their region, but usually did not interact with tribes from other regions. They did, however, have some contact with the Olmecs of the Gulf coast, the Mixtecs of Oaxaca, and the *pochteca*, the Aztec traveling merchants of Tenochtitlán. This was a region rich in cacao and other natural resources sought by the people of Mexico's central valley. One of the early cities of importance in this southern region was Izapa, located in the coastal lowland region of Chiapas. Another was Kaminaljuyu.

The Classic Maya

Sometime around A.D. 250 or 300, some of the people who have come to be known as the Maya moved down from the highlands into the jungles of northern Guatemala, in what is known as the Petén region. Exactly why they moved is unknown, although it may have had something to do with the need for more land for people and crops. Here they began to develop large cities and a fascinating culture uniquely their own. This period (A.D. 300–900) is known as the Classic Period of Maya culture.

Trade was a vital part of life in the Mayan cities of the Petén lowlands. Some of the main trade routes were along such rivers as the Usumacinta, which flowed north into the central valley of Mexico. Others followed the highlands in the west, the region that the Maya had left. The Petén jungle lacked many of the resources that the highlands were rich in, so these resources had to be imported to the Petén cities of the Classic Period. Obsidian and flint for making knives and other tools, and even the large volcanic stones used for grinding maize, had to be transported down the mountains and through the jungle.

Other imports from the highlands included the feathers of the quetzal bird. These feathers were difficult to come by, and, therefore, were highly prized. In addition, the beautiful, green color of the feathers was sacred to most Mesoamerican peoples. The feathers were made into head-dresses and capes that were worn by priests or leaders.

The Pacific lowlands, which the Maya had vacated even earlier than the highlands, also remained an important part of the trading network. From this region they received cacao beans, which they could use for trade with other tribes. Other coastal products that the Maya traded for included salt, dried fish, shells, and stingray spines, which were used as needles for piercing ears and in rituals of self-sacrifice.

The Maya of Palenque traded with, and were influenced by, the native peoples of Teotihuacán. A palace complex with a three-story observatory can be seen in Palenque today.

Roads of limestone blocks were constructed along trade routes in some places, while dirt footpaths existed in others. Porters who transported the Mayan goods found the dirt paths easier on their bare feet. Like the Aztecs and other natives of Mexico, the Maya had neither beasts of burden nor wheeled vehicles to help them.

Tikal became a great ceremonial city in the Petén region. Here the Maya built huge temple pyramids, among the tallest in the Americas. Another important Mayan city of this time was Palenque (in what is now Chiapas, Mexico). Located in the northern part of the Maya's realm, it was heavily influenced by trade with Teotihuacán. Copán (in what is now Honduras) was a vital city located at the southern edge of Mayan territory. It was probably an important center for trade with the natives of the Panama region, to the south, who were skilled in metalwork.

There were also trade routes to the northeast, which connected the central Mayan cities with northern lowland cities on the Yucatán Peninsula. One of these cities was Cobá. Honey and salt were among its items offered for trade.

The Rise of the Yucatán

One of the great mysteries of archaeology involves the collapse of the Classic Mayan culture. For a number of reasons, the Maya began to desert their Petén-area cities between the years A.D. 800 and 900. This exodus may have occurred because the farms and forests could not support the number of people in the area. Perhaps these cities had to import more than they were able to export. Rivalries between cities may have intensified and escalated into devastating wars. Whatever the case may be, the Mayan cities of the Yucatán area now became dominant. This period in Mayan history (A.D. 900 to 1500) is called the Post-Classic Period.

The Maya of the Yucatán were heavily influenced by tribes from Mexico, mainly the Toltecs. Legend says that the great Quetzalcoatl, called Kukulcan by the Maya, led a group of Toltecs to the Yucatán after the fall of Tula.

One of the principal cities of the Yucatán was Chichén Itzá. It had one of the largest marketplaces. In its Court of a Thousand Columns, many hundreds of people gathered to barter for food, pottery, tools, and slaves. Most of the slaves were people who had been captured during wars with other Mayan cities.

By the end of the twelfth century, Mayapan was the dominant city. It seems that Mayapan demanded tribute from other Mayan cities, but they did not comply. Fighting between various clans or groups increased, and in 1441, Mayapan was destroyed. The Mayan people broke up into many small groups, and lived in villages scattered throughout the Yucatán and Petén regions.

At the marketplace in Chichén Itzá, called the Court of a Thousand Columns, people traded items for crafts, food, and slaves.

The Maya who stayed in the Yucatán still had a very valuable commodity to trade—salt. Canoes as long as fifty feet could carry trade goods by water around the Yucatán Peninsula. These canoes would stay close to the shore, and would be filled with such goods as obsidian, raw copper, and woven textiles from central Mexico and the Gulf coast. These things would be traded for honey and salt in the Yucatán. Traders would then go farther south, to Honduras, to trade for axes. The island of Cozumel was a popular place to visit. Not only was it important as a religious shrine, but it was known for its large supplies of honey.

The Maya considered jade to be precious and created ceremonial objects from it, such as this mask that was discovered in Palenque.

The Spanish Invaders

When Christopher Columbus made his fourth and last voyage, he met a Mayan trading canoe off the coast of Honduras. It was 1502, and the Maya's first encounter with Europeans. Columbus noted the finely woven cloth, the capes of beautiful feathers, the bells and knives of copper, and the food that the canoe contained. Then he sailed on, still looking for a passage to the Indies.

In 1517, an expedition led by the Spaniard Francisco Hernandez de Cordoba landed on the Yucatán Peninsula. He offered the Maya some green beads, which they thought were jade, a stone more precious to them than gold. In return, the Maya gave the Spaniards gold objects in the shape of birds and fish. The Spaniards must have been very pleased, since gold meant wealth to them, and finding gold meant fame. They did not know that the gold for these objects had come from far away from the Yucatán.

Reports of the visits by bearded strangers traveled from Mayan village to village. Now, in addition to the considerable amount of intertribal fighting that was going on at this time, there would be battles fought with the Spanish. Also, thousands of Maya would die in epidemics of diseases such as smallpox brought over by the Europeans. By the mid-1540s, the Spanish had control of the Yucatán, although they did not defeat the Lake Petén Itza Maya until 1697.

Isolated groups of Maya continued to rebel against the Spanish throughout the following centuries. The majestic Mayan cities were abandoned or destroyed. The Maya's books were burned, and their art was stolen. It was the end of a civilization that had endured for a thousand years.

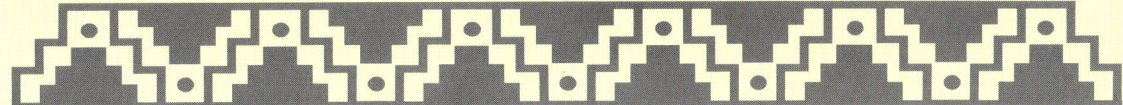

Mayan Trade Today

The Spanish may have brought about the end of the Mayan civilization, but they did not destroy the Mayan people. Many still live in the Mexican and Guatemalan highlands. They raise crops that they sell in the cities for things they need. Maize, beans, and squash remain the primary crops with which they feed their families.

The women still weave beautiful Mayan designs into the fabrics they make. As in the days of old, market days are times for lively discussion and active trade.

Mayan people today still sell and exchange beautiful crafts to obtain the things that they need. Here, a Mayan woman does traditional embroidery.

The Spanish took over the cultivation of cacao, and grew other crops that did well in the tropical climate, such as bananas and coffee. The Maya who did not retreat into the jungle were forced to work on the plantations and in the mines. Some were sent as slaves to Caribbean islands.

Chapter 4

The Caribbean

Researchers believe that the first peoples to live in the Caribbean islands arrived in canoes from South America, Central America, or Florida. These early peoples lived in caves and survived on wild food they could hunt or gather.

People of the Islands

Sometime around 900 B.C., a group of South American natives called the Arawaks began to leave their homeland in what is now Venezuela. Over a period of several hundred years, they made their way out into the Caribbean Sea in dugouts they called *canoas,* from which the word "canoe" comes. Settling first in Trinidad, they eventually moved northward in search of new island homesites. The sea offered turtles, crabs, and fish for eating, a diet that they supplemented with manioc (or cassava) roots, sweet potatoes, maize, and peanuts that they grew in small farm plots. The Arawaks also harvested cotton, which they could weave into cloth, although there was little need for clothing in this tropical paradise. They made carvings of wood, bone, stone, and seashell. They also produced a very distinctive form of

*Opposite:
A Taino descendant builds a strong canoe using traditional methods. The Taino traveled by canoe from South America to the Caribbean.*

Food and carvings, such as this stone belt, were used for trade by the Taino.

pottery that they had learned to make in South America. Study of their pottery has enabled archaeologists to trace the routes by which they moved from island to island.

By A.D. 1000, the Arawaks had settled on the northern islands of the Caribbean, including those known today as Cuba, Hispaniola, and the Bahamas. These Arawaks of the northern Caribbean came to be known as the Taino. Their only enemy was a native group called the Caribs, also descendants of those Arawaks who had left their Venezuelan homeland many centuries before.

While the Taino tended to be peaceful, friendly people, the Caribs developed a much more aggressive society. Carib raiders, their faces smeared with black war paint, were greatly feared by the Taino. They were known to attack Taino villages in the stillness of the night, killing the men and carrying off the women.

The Caribs, as well as other island peoples, used canoes hollowed out from huge trees to travel around their islands and to other nearby islands. Some of their canoes were large enough to hold up to a hundred people. They traded the food they grew and the things they made with friendly neighbors.

In some of the streams on their islands, they found bits of a soft yellow metal—gold. They pounded this metal into jewelry that they wore in their nose and ears. Sometimes they would trade the pieces of gold or the jewelry, but no group ever accumulated a particularly large amount of it.

The End of an Era

A group of Taino who lived on an island that they called Guanahaní were the first to see the three great ships—the *Niña,* the *Pinta,* and the *Santa María*—on October 12, 1492. Although the strangers who landed on the shore of their island must have looked very strange to the Taino—with their pale skin, bearded faces, and heavy clothing—the Taino were courteous hosts.

The captain of the ships was Christopher Columbus. He had told the king and queen of Spain that he could find a shortcut to "the Indies" (China, Japan, and India) by sailing west from Europe. Because Columbus was sure that the island he had found was off the coast of Asia, he called the people there Indians.

When men from Columbus's three ships arrived at Caribbean islands, they exchanged gifts with the Taino.

The Taino traded gifts with the strangers. Columbus gave them red caps, little copper bells, and glass beads. In return, they gave the Spaniards cotton thread, food, and pet parrots. When they saw that Columbus was most interested in their jewelry, they tried to tell him that not much of the gold that it was made of came from their island, but from trading with other islanders. The Taino gladly showed the strangers how to get to the other islands.

The Europeans, however, did not intend to trade with the Taino or other island peoples. They came, instead, as conquerors. They soon claimed all the land of the islands for themselves to establish a "New Spain." They expected the natives to adopt their religion and to work for them. When the natives did not do so willingly, they were beaten or killed. Others died from the hard labor that they were forced to do, and from European diseases that they had never been exposed to before. By 1550, the Taino had ceased to exist as a separate people; they had either died of abuse or disease, or had been absorbed into the Spanish culture.

As time went on, the Spaniards set up colonies on the Caribbean islands, and from there they explored yet other parts of the so-called New World. The islands became the link between Spain and its colonies. They served as stop-overs, where people could plan the rest of their journeys, and adjust to the climate, before moving on to other ports. It was here that the conquistadores also purchased the supplies they needed—meat, wine, clothes, weapons, and ammunition, among other things—before setting off for Mexico and Panama. When the Indians of the islands were all dead or gone, the colonists imported Africans to work as slaves on the sugarcane plantations they had established there. Eventually, the Africans would win their freedom, and today their descendants make up the majority of inhabitants of the islands.

The People of the Northern Coast of South America

On Christopher Columbus's third voyage, he sailed between the island of Trinidad and the coast of what is now called Venezuela. Along this coast he saw natives with strings of pearls around their necks. He traded for large quantities of the valuable pearls on the Venezuelan island of Margarita.

Soon other Spanish sailors were busily investigating the northern coast of South America. In 1494, Alonso de Ojeda sailed into the Gulf of Maracaibo and saw a native village built on stilts, to avoid damage from floods. He called it "Little Venice"—or Venezuela. De Ojeda took any treasure he could find in the village before sailing on.

During the next few years, the Europeans found in the forests of northern South America numerous groups of Arawak- and Carib-speaking peoples. At first, most of these natives were friendly toward the Europeans. They willingly traded their food and water and their gold and pearls for the iron tools and trinkets that they were offered. In fact, many of the Europeans would have died of starvation if they had not been given food by the natives.

Soon, however, the Spaniards began raiding the coastal villages for slaves to replace those natives on the islands who were dying. Instead of trading, they simply took whatever treasure they could find. In many places, the native people responded with bows and poisoned arrows.

In 1520, Gonzalo de Ocampo founded New Toledo (near the present-day city of Cumaná, Venezuela). All of the settlers, however, were killed by natives once de Ocampo sailed away. Two years later, de Ocampo tried again on the same spot, and Cumaná became the first permanent colonial settlement on the South American continent.

The Europeans often established their trading posts in coastal harbors and at the mouths of rivers. The natives of the region had long used these same harbors and rivers as part of their trading networks that went both south into the Amazon rainforest and north into the Caribbean islands.

Because the Spanish tended to think of the Arawaks as their friends and the Caribs as their enemies, they were willing to trade with the Arawaks and to fight against the Caribs. Sometimes the Arawaks even used their friendship with the Spaniards to instigate wars with the Caribs. This association with the Spanish actually had a negative effect on the Arawaks, as they were forced to abandon their way of life and to depend even more on the Spanish, and they became increasingly exposed to European diseases.

Meanwhile, the Spaniards were not the only ones searching for treasure in the New World. The Dutch were also heavily involved in trade with various places along the northern coast of South America in the 1600s. They imported cotton, raw sugar, and tobacco from their trading posts, and sent back to Holland refined sugar and textiles made from the cotton. The English and the French also competed for trade resources along the Caribbean coast.

A little farther to the west of Venezuela was the land that would one day be known as Colombia. From its coastal lowlands to the valleys and plateaus at the northern end of the Andes lived many groups of people.

One of these was the Muisca, a branch of the Chibcha group, who lived in this corner of the Caribbean world. The Muisca lived in the plateaus of the region around the present-day city of Bogotá. They had a well-organized society and had conquered many of their neighbors. They grew maize and other crops. They had only a small amount of gold in their territory; but they had something worth more than gold: salt (salt is essential for proper nutrition). They were able to trade bricks of salt to other natives for all the gold they wanted.

The People of Central America

The Cuna traded goods among themselves and with local tribes. Today, people come from around the world to buy the embroidered molas of the Cuna.

There were many tribes that made the strip of land between South America and Mexico their home. Unlike the Maya and the natives of Mexico, these people grew very little maize. Instead, their diet more closely resembled that of the Caribbean islanders and the people of northern South America. They grew sweet potatoes and manioc, which do well in humid lowlands.

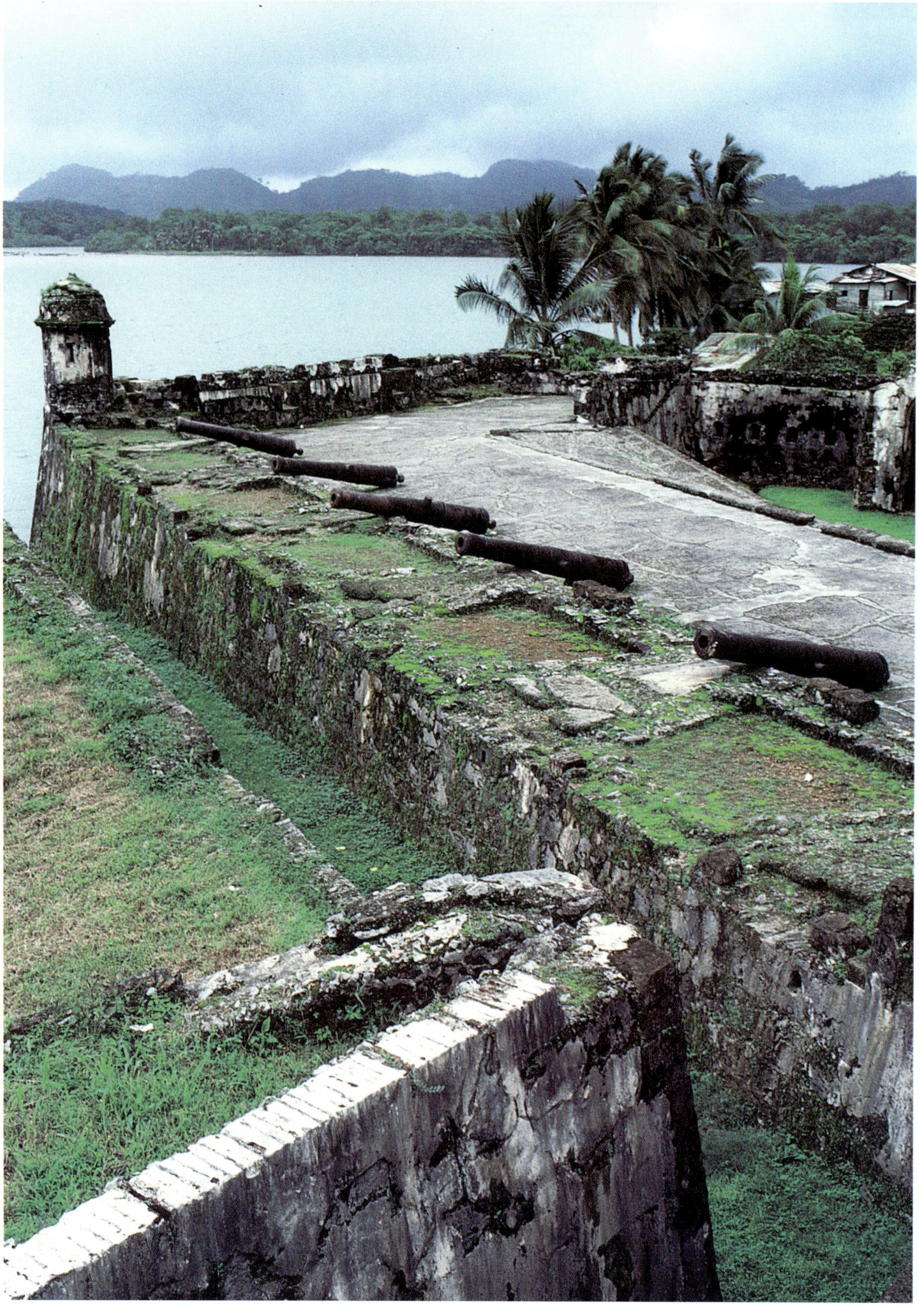

The Cuna Indians were an important group of people in this region. They lived throughout the area of what is now Panama. (There were probably also Caribs and Chibcha in this area at one time.) The Cuna participated extensively in trade, mainly traveling by canoe along the long Caribbean coast of Central America and northwestern South America. Trade went on between the mainland Cuna and those who lived on the offshore islands, and between the Cuna and neighboring tribes. They may have traded as far south as the land of the Inca in the Andes, and as far north as the land of the Maya.

On Columbus's fourth voyage, after having seen the Mayan traders off the coast of Honduras, he traded with some Guaymi Indians, who lived along the Caribbean coast of Panama. He gave them beads and red caps in return for their lovely gold necklaces.

As more Spanish soldiers and treasure seekers arrived, this narrow strip of land between the two oceans became strategically important. It was a perfect starting point for expeditions down the Pacific coast of South America. A number of colonists made a living by supplying sailors and soldiers who were traveling between Spain and Peru with goods they needed.

The city of Portobelo became famous for the business it attracted to its annual fairs. For forty days, merchants from all over the region gathered to sell and trade goods of all sorts. In 1739, however, the British Navy destroyed the city of Portobelo, thus ending the fairs.

Present-day Guaymi Indians have largely retreated to secluded highland villages, but the Cuna of Panama continue to be active traders. They sell coconuts in the markets of small villages, and in such big cities as Panama City. People come from all over the world to buy the beautiful *molas*, or colorful embroidered fabrics, that the women make.

Opposite: Merchants would travel to Portobelo to participate in the city's famous fairs. Fort San Lorenzo, seen here, once protected the important trade city.

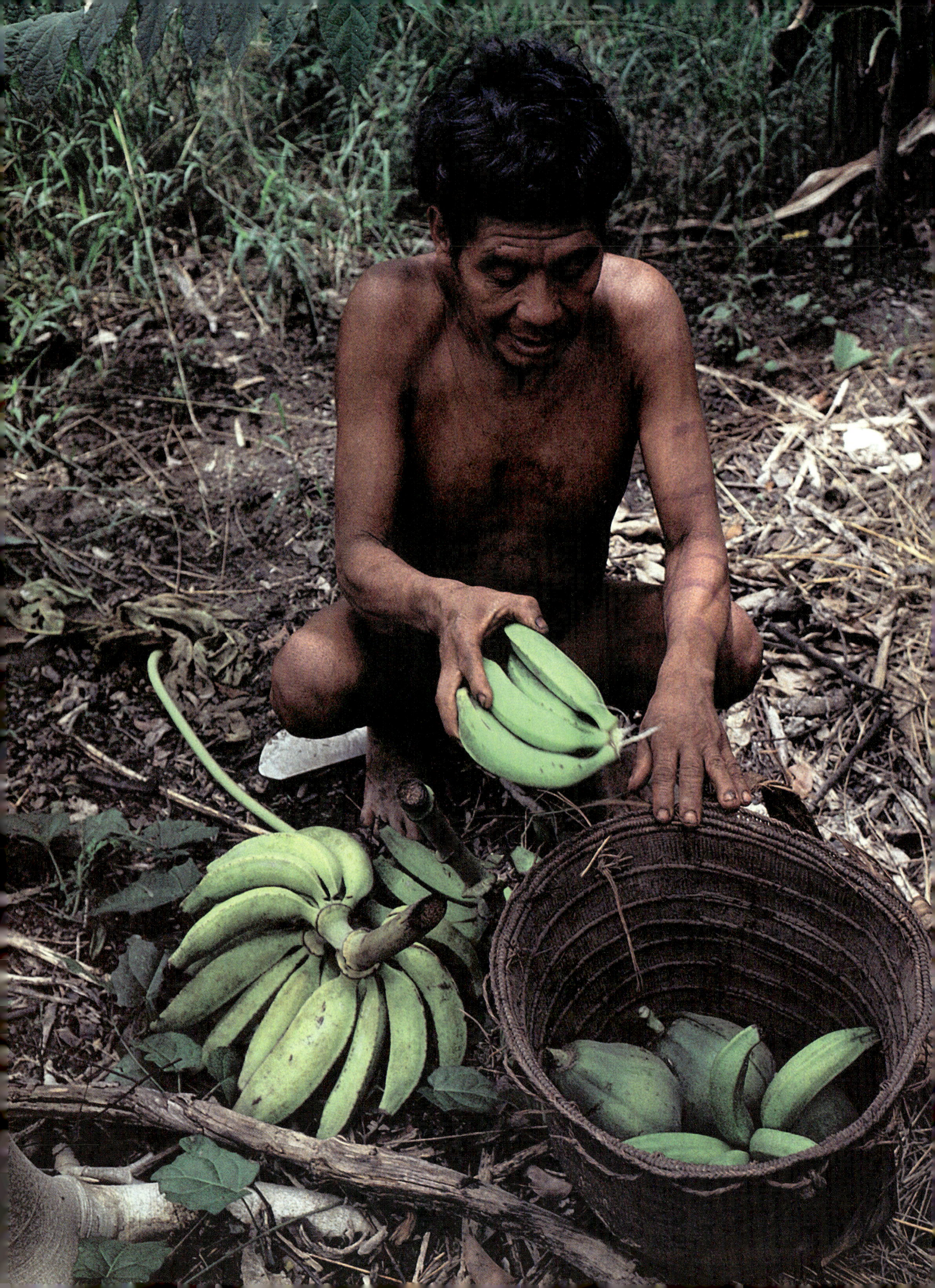

Chapter

5

The Amazon Basin

Archaeologists believe that there were people living in the region around the Amazon River, known as the Amazon Basin, as long ago as 2000 B.C. Such estimates are difficult to make, however, because of the warm, wet climate of the area, which decomposes the remains of ancient cultures and leaves few traces for researchers to study. Some recent studies suggest that the hunter-gatherers of the Amazon are *recent* arrivals—living there for hundreds, rather than thousands, of years. Nonetheless, this area is one of the few in the world where people can be found whose way of life has changed very little since their ancestors first made it their home. Thus, instead of the remains of ancient cultures, scientists have the opportunity to study existing people, living in ancestral ways.

The First Amazonians

The rivers and forests of the Amazon Basin supported a great variety of plant and animal life. Some plants were edible, while others could be used to build shelters. Some of the fish could be eaten; other, poisonous ones gave a lethal edge to weapons. Without metal for tools, and with very little stone, these natives made points for their arrows

*Opposite:
A Yanomami man fills a basket with plantains for his family.*

A man fishes in a tributary of the Amazon River. Natives of the Amazon Basin survived by using everything they found in nature.

and nails for their homes of hardwood. These people used in some way virtually everything they found in nature.

They acquired food by hunting, fishing, and gathering. They cleared small garden spaces in the jungle by chopping down large trees and burning away the ground cover. This is called the slash-and-burn method. They planted a few crops, including manioc, maize, sweet potatoes, and peanuts. Because the nutrients in the soil in this region were quickly depleted, people were forced to move their gardens every few years and repeat the process. Each group, therefore, had to have access to large amounts of land, which the Amazon Basin certainly offered. The poor-quality soil kept villages small. In places where the soil was exceptionally fertile and able to support intensive agriculture, larger villages sometimes formed.

Despite the poor soil, the natives were able to produce large amounts of food. Many other foods, such as turtles, fish, and small mammals were also available. A visitor in the 1600s wrote, "These Indians never know what hunger is."

The people of the Amazon Basin believed that the world was full of spirits, some good and some evil. They believed anyone from outside their village was a potential enemy. One group was always worried about the possibility of attack from another group. Sometimes one group would attack another just to keep from being attacked first.

In the Amazon, maintaining a community was a group process. Here, a young Yanomami weaves leaves to thatch his family's house.

A result of this was that each community had to be as self-sufficient as possible. Community members pooled their resources so that each person had enough to survive. A system of feasting and gift exchange also developed; people who feasted together were less likely to attack each other. Thus certain villages took turns inviting other villages to huge feasts. Along with the feast, the host village offered other items as gifts to its guests. The more food and gifts the host village could present to its guests, the more prestige it gained. It was even better if there was enough food left over for the guests to take home. The guest village was then expected to reciprocate. A group of people who could not hold a feast and give gifts was considered weak, and would probably be raided by a stronger group.

Villages that participated in feasting and gift exchange might do other trading. Some of the items traded might include arrow shafts and points, cotton threads and woven cotton cloth, and hammocks and baskets made from vines.

Foreign Traders Bring Change

One of the first Europeans to reach the mouth of the Amazon River was Vicente Yáñez Pinzón, a Spaniard who sailed a short way up the river in 1500. Just a few months later, the Portuguese admiral Pedro Alvares Cabral spotted the mountains along the eastern coast of Brazil. He became the first European to land in South America south of the Amazon, and he is usually given credit for "discovering" Brazil.

Alvares Cabral stayed in Brazil for only a few days. The Tupi tribe, in whose territory he had landed, were extremely friendly, and they allowed him to take fresh water and food for his journey. As a result of this brief visit, and in accordance with a treaty signed by Spain and Portugal dividing the unexplored parts of the New World between them, the Portuguese would claim the right to colonize Brazil.

Whereas Spain came primarily to conquer the New World, Portugal came to trade. Its first construction was a wharf and a site where products were displayed. Colonization was slow, as Portuguese merchants were at first more interested in the Spice Islands (the Moluccas) they reached by traveling around Africa, and in the mines on the African continent itself. French adventurers began to land along Brazil's coast to ship back to France loads of the large trees known as brazilwood. The Dutch sent merchants into the region to search for such products as cinnamon and cacao.

When the king of Portugal heard rumors that silver had been found south of the Amazon, he realized that he might lose much of value if he did not stake a serious claim in the New World. Gradually, trading posts and small Portuguese settlements were built along the coast. In 1532, Martin de Sousa founded São Vincente, the first permanent colony in Brazil. For much of the next hundred years, the Portuguese colonists would compete with other Europeans for control of the brazilwood and other resources of Brazil.

All of this activity among the European powers had a devastating effect on the natives of the Amazon region. At first they traded their labor, cutting and hauling trees to shore in return for metal axes and such European items as combs and clothing. When the natives felt that they had amassed enough of these objects, they quit working. The Europeans, in turn, quit trading for their labor. Instead, they provoked wars in which captives were enslaved. Many of the Tupi, who were among the first Amazonian peoples to have regular contact with the Portuguese colonists, died of European disease or were enslaved.

There were no obvious riches for the Europeans to steal from the people of Amazonia, who had very little gold, silver, or other precious metals. What the Europeans stole instead was their land—and their very lives. Many of the natives, in an effort to escape sickness and those trying to enslave them, chose to move ever deeper into the forest, away from the strangers and the strange ways. There are places in this great jungle where such peoples, still hiding from the strangers, live today.

In the early 1700s, there were several significant gold strikes in Brazil. Natives, and then imported Africans, were forced to work in the mines. From the 1700s on, some rubber was exported from the Amazon region, mainly for use in waterproofing. It had only a limited market, however, until 1837, when Charles Goodyear discovered a process called vulcanization, which produced weatherproof rubber. By 1840, the Brazilian rubber business was booming. While a few rubber barons became wealthy, thousands of natives were forced to work in virtual slavery in the gathering and smoking of the rubber.

The search for resources to remove from the Amazon Basin continued through the nineteenth century and still occurs to some extent today. In recent decades, deposits of

The Kaipo live in a traditional village deep in the Amazon rainforest.

iron ore, nickel, tin, and copper have been found in the Amazon Basin. People are no longer forced to work as slaves in these industries, but there is great concern about how overdevelopment will affect the delicately balanced environment and the lifestyles of the native peoples who still live there.

Cultures at the Crossroads

Since the Europeans first arrived in the Amazon Basin, the native peoples have been faced with the problem of how to react. The Waorani of Ecuador and the Yanomami of Venezuela and Brazil are examples of two groups of Amazon Basin natives currently struggling to deal with the influence of the modern world.

The Waorani's first contact with Europeans came in the 1600s, when some of them were captured and enslaved. In the 1800s, rubber gatherers invaded their territory. Again, some natives were forced to work for the invaders. In the 1940s, the discovery of oil brought the strangers once again. In recent decades, missionaries have been working with the Waorani, trying to keep the peace among rival Waorani and with outsiders. Some Waorani have adopted present-day ways and are using modern tools and wearing contemporary clothing. Others, however, remain firmly set in the traditional ways.

First contact for the Yanomami came a little later, but they are facing many of the same dilemmas as the Waorani. For a long time, they resisted the presence of gold hunters, missionaries, and all other strangers in their territory. Some Yanomami continue this resistance today, while others attend schools where they learn skills such as reading, sewing, and modern cooking.

As the general population of the countries of South America increases, there is also increased pressure to develop the rainforest—the last refuge of the Waorani, the Yanomami, and other native groups. Some areas are cleared of trees and other plants to make way for roads, cities, and mines. In other places, it is farms and ranches that crowd out the forests and the forest dwellers.

As more and more of the rainforest disappears, however, there are those who are taking steps to stop the destruction. Many companies are looking for ways to use products of the rainforest, such as fruits, nuts, and medicines, without destroying it. Some companies are also looking for ways to share the profits of these businesses with the native peoples of the region.

A few people are even beginning to realize that although there is much that we can teach the natives of the Amazon, there is also a lot that they can teach us. We could also learn from them about living in harmony with our environment so that one generation does not destroy it for the next. We could learn to live more simply and find out that there are better ways to eat (such as consuming less meat, which would mean less land needed for ranches). We could also learn that there are more ways to define "riches" than just the number of goods we own.

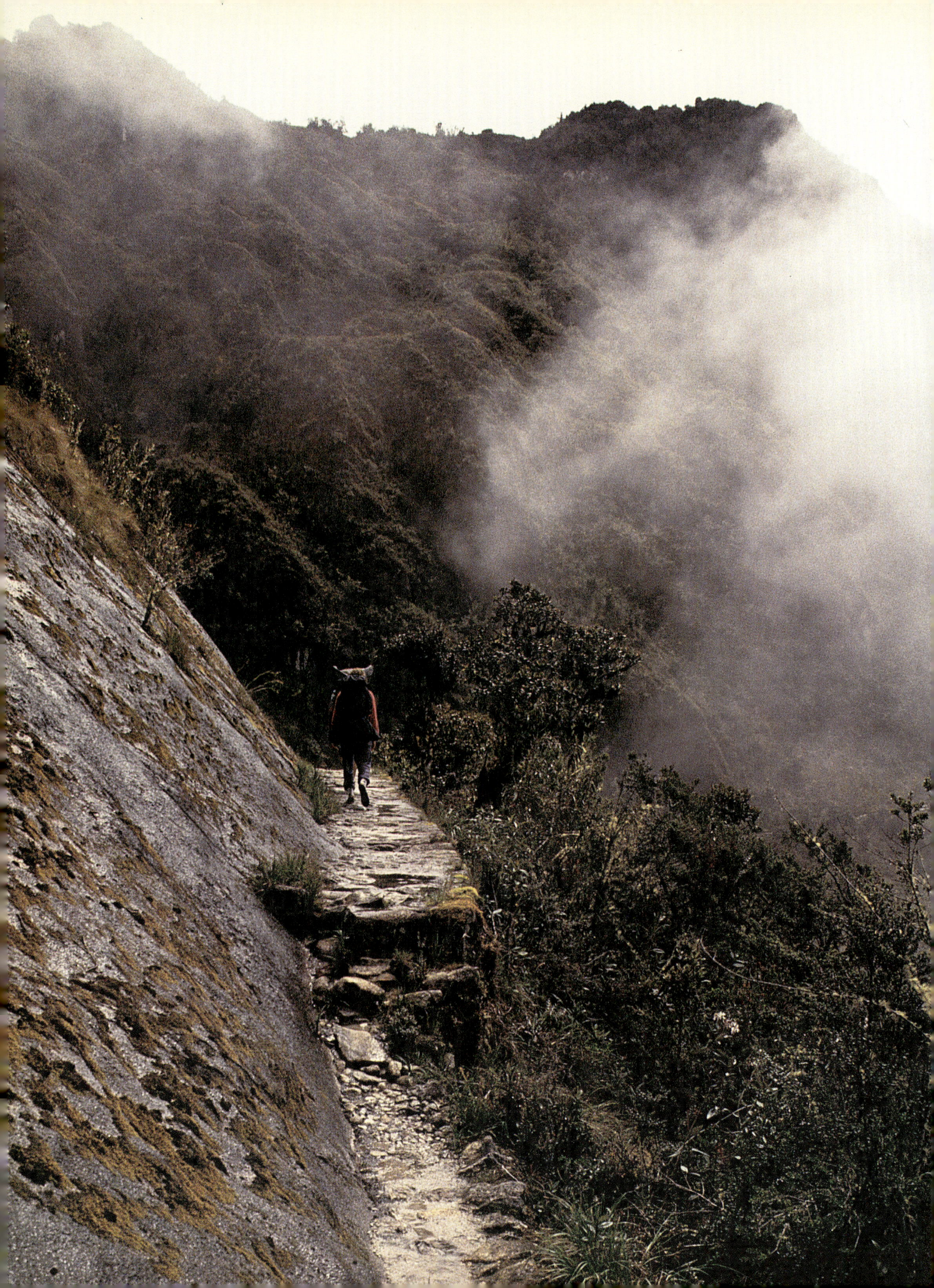

Chapter

6

The Andes

Between the years 1000 B.C. and A.D. 1000, there were numerous groups of people living in the Andes mountains. Where the soil was fertile, they lived primarily by farming. Where there were large bodies of water, they harvested food from the lakes and the sea. Many of them found that by trading with their neighbors, all were able to achieve a better life. Some groups became more aggressive than others and increased the size of their territories and their access to goods by conquering their neighbors.

One of the earliest groups to develop an identifiable culture was that of the Chavín. Around 900 B.C., these people built temples and homes decorated with stone carvings of snakes, birds, and jaguars. They also worked in metal, creating jewelry and religious objects in gold.

Another group, called the Moche, lived in the northern part of what is now Peru during the first millennium. These people were farmers who supplemented their diet with food from the sea. They probably traded the produce they raised (including maize, beans, and potatoes) for sea lions, fish, and edible seaweed from the inhabitants of the coast. In

*Opposite:
A hiker walks along an Incan trail in the Andes. The Inca built these trails to connect their cities and to have a way to transport goods.*

A Mochica cacao bag is an example of this culture's artistic talent. Artwork was traded for other goods.

addition, people along the shore collected bird droppings, called guano, which the farmers farther inland used as fertilizer. The farmers, in turn, grew cotton, the threads of which fishermen used for their nets.

The Moche made seaworthy rafts by tying large bundles of reeds together. Besides gathering food from the sea, Mochica seamen probably used these rafts to trade with other groups of people farther along the coast.

The Moche also went up into the mountains for wood from the forests and for minerals such as gold and silver. They had contact with other people in the Andes, contact that sometimes took the form of friendly trading and other times gave way to military conquest. The Moche made a distinctive type of pottery, and its remains have been found across a broad range of territory. Archaeologists believe that this pottery, as well as Mochica beliefs and traditions, was spread primarily as the result of their success as warriors.

The Inca

Eventually, one group of people would rise to power and claim a great deal of the Andes mountains for their own. These people have come to be known as the Inca. Originally, however, they called themselves the Quechua. The Supreme Inca was their leader and was believed to be descended from the sun. The Inca also held that Manco

Capac, the first Inca, was instructed by the sun god to go forth and find a place from which to teach the worship of the sun. The place that Manco Capac found (around the year A.D. 1200) became the city of Cuzco, and the people he taught were the Quechua. Manco Capac and his descendants were supreme rulers over these people. Each ruler increased the amount of territory he governed. Over time, all of the people were called Inca.

In the late 1400s, under the leadership of Tupa Inca, the empire included territory from what is now the northern border of Ecuador all the way to what is now central Chile. From the capital city of Cuzco, the Inca governed approximately 6 million people.

Only a portion of what the Inca collected from the people they conquered went to Cuzco. Most of it was distributed throughout the empire directly from the areas in which it was collected. This distribution required large administrative staffs. The Inca did not have great markets where individuals bartered for their own needs. Instead, the government took responsibility for ensuring that people's needs were met. There were government storehouses from which items were distributed. In return, people would labor at designated tasks. Thus, the kind of trade that flourished in Mexico was very limited in the Andes. The government had strict control over the distribution of goods from various parts of the empire. A person had to have the Supreme Inca's permission to possess luxury items, and that permission was given only to a select few. Agricultural produce such as maize and cotton from lowland farms were brought to government storehouses in the mountains. They were exchanged for potatoes and minerals, which were sent back to the lowlands.

As might be expected, Cuzco was a very carefully controlled city. There were only a few ways into and out of the

A guardhouse outside the Incan city of Machu Picchu was used to monitor travel and trade in and out of the city.

city, and these were well guarded. All trips required a permit, and no one was let into the city after dark.

One reason for the empire's success was that the Inca were great organizers. Goods and laborers were used as efficiently as possible throughout the empire. Every able person was expected to work. There was no need for money, because everything was provided for by the government. All debts to the government were paid for in work or in the products of work. The only one who owned anything was the Supreme Inca, and he owned everything.

To make the distribution of goods easier, the Inca constructed an impressive system of roads. Suspension bridges were built over deep mountain gorges. Human runners sped along these roads, carrying messages and bundles of goods. About every ten miles along the roads were rest houses for the runners, and storehouses filled with both local produce and imports from other parts of the empire. It is said that a relay system of runners could carry items from the Inca capital of Cuzco to the northern city of Quito, a distance of 1,000 miles through the mountains, in about a week.

Llamas were important to the Inca trading network. Llamas could carry one hundred pounds of goods up and down the mountains, thereby increasing the amount of goods any one group of people could transport. This was also a great advantage to the Inca army, in that its soldiers were kept well supplied. The Inca were the only native people of the New World to use a beast of burden.

Most Inca worked on small plots of land that provided some of their food needs. Their main crops were potatoes and maize, but they also cultivated sweet potatoes, bananas, peanuts, tobacco, beans, and fruits. Surplus food and supplemental food (food that could not be grown in a particular region) was kept in government storehouses, and given out to those in need and to those who had earned it. Wool and llama meat from the mountains were sent to the coast, and maize, fish, and cotton were brought from the coastal lowlands to the mountains. Those who raised cotton or sheared wool from llamas, vicuñas, and alpacas took it to government warehouses. It was then distributed to others for weaving into cloth.

Metals, such as copper, gold, silver, and tin, were mined in the Andes mountains. Tin and copper were melted together to make bronze. Metal tools were made in molds, but ceremonial objects of gold and silver were artfully shaped by hand.

Thanks to the Inca's efficient distribution system and advanced farming methods, there was usually plenty of food for everyone. Inca in the Andes used terraced farming to prevent erosion of the mountainsides and fertilized their fields with guano imported from the coast. From time to time, they carried large amounts of soil up the mountainsides to replenish their fields. Along the dry western coast, they dug canals and reservoirs and transported water from the mountains via aqueducts.

Incan gold objects, such as this gold cup, were crafted by hand and owned only by the elite.

Inca in Colonial Times

In 1532, the Spanish conquistador Francisco Pizarro captured and later killed the Inca emperor Atahualpa, and established himself as the governor of Peru. Even though bands of Inca continued to fight for many years, they were for the most part enslaved and badly treated. They were forced to carry goods from the sea coast to the cities that grew up in the mountains around the mines. They also worked on the plantations where food was grown to feed the colonists.

Sometimes the natives were paid for their labor in trade goods. However, this effort at fairness on the part of the Europeans was often abused, and some mine owners insisted that the natives accept goods that they did not need, such as razors when they had no beards, and silk stockings when they wore no shoes.

With the riches that they took from the Inca mines, the Europeans were able to import the finest goods from the farthest corners of the world. German ironware, Dutch linens, Egyptian rugs, Chinese ivory, and French beaver hats were transported to the mountains of Peru and Bolivia.

Despite the fact that they lost control of their empire, many of the Inca continued to think of themselves as a separate people. In the minds of many of the inhabitants of the Andes mountains today, some of whom are the descendants of the people confronted by Pizarro and his men, they are still Inca, children of the sun.

Glossary

anthropologists Scientists who study the relationships between living peoples, their environment, and their culture. Anthropologists try to understand how people live and work, what they believe, and how their values shape their society.

aqueduct A pipe, or canal, used for transporting water.

archaeologists Scientists who study the material remains of past human life and activities. Archaeologists often excavate the ruins of ancient civilizations and study the objects they find.

cacao beans Products of the cacao tree, which grows in tropical climates. The natives of Mexico crushed the beans and mixed them with water to produce a chocolate drink. They also used the beans like money when trading for other items.

canoa An Arawak word meaning "canoe."

causeway A bridge, or road, over water or marshland.

chinampas Plots of land created by the Aztecs by fencing in a marshy area and filling it with mud or dirt.

chocolatl Chocolate; a drink made from cacao beans.

conquistador A conqueror; particularly a soldier or an explorer from Spain.

guano Bird droppings, used for fertilizer.

hacienda A large plantation or ranch. In colonial Mexico, haciendas were owned by the Spaniards.

maize A small, grassy plant that we now know as corn. Originally with only a couple of kernels per plant, it grew wild in Mexico and was cultivated by early people.

manioc A root plant, also known as cassava, that grows in tropical climates. Manioc is poisonous unless it is prepared properly. Natives squeezed the manioc to remove the poisonous juices then baked and dried the manioc "cakes."

metallurgist A person who extracts metal from its ore and creates other objects with it.

mola An embroidered piece of fabric traditionally made by the Cuna women of Panama.

pochteca A hereditary merchant class among the Aztecs.

pre-Columbian A term referring to events in the Americas before 1492, the year of the arrival of Christopher Columbus in the New World and the beginning of the European invasion.

reductions Small, poor native communities in New Spain in the seventeenth century.

sombrero A large hat that shades much of the face.

terraced farming Multiple layers of flat strips of ground gradually moving up or down the side of a hill, preventing erosion, or the washing away of the soil of the hillside.

tribute A payment, or tax, given to a ruler.

Further Reading

Berdan, Frances F. *The Aztecs.* New York: Chelsea House Publishers, 1989.

Clay, Rebecca. *Native Latin American Cultures: The Arts.* Vero Beach, FL: Rourke Publications, Inc., 1995.

Jacobs, Francine. *The Tainos.* New York: Putnam's Sons, 1992.

Kendall, Sarita. *Worlds of the Past: The Incas.* New York: New Discovery Books, 1991.

Lucas, Eileen. *Native Latin American Cultures: European Conquest.* Vero Beach, FL: Rourke Publications, Inc., 1995.

McCall, Barbara. *Native American Culture: Daily Life.* Vero Beach, FL: Rourke Publications, Inc., 1994.

Sattler, Helen Roney. *The Earliest Americans.* New York: Clarion Books, 1993.

Sherrow, Victoria. *Native Latin American Cultures: Daily Customs.* Vero Beach, FL: Rourke Publications, Inc., 1995.

Siy, Alexandra. *The Waorani.* New York: Dillon Press, 1993.

Sullivan, George. *Treasure Hunt: The Sixteen-Year Search for the Lost Treasure Ship Atocha.* New York: Henry Holt & Co., 1987.

Index

A
Alvares Cabral, Pedro, 48
Arawak tribe, 35–36, 39, 40
Atahualpa, 58
Aztecs, 19–20, 24–25
  marketplace of, 22–24
  merchants of, 20–22

B
Brazilwood, 48

C
Cabeza de Vaca, Alvar Nunez, 10–11
Canoes
  Arawak, 35
  Aztec, 19
  Mayan, 31
Carib tribe, 36, 39, 40
Chavin tribe, 53
Chibcha group, of Muisca tribe, 40
Chichén Itzá, 30, 31 (photo)
Chinampas, 19
Chocolatl, 21
Columbus, Christopher, 32, 37–39
Copper Canyon, 7 (photo)
Copper jewelry, 11
Cordoba, Francisco Hernandez de, 32
Corn. See Maize.
Cortés, Hernando, 23, 24–25
Court of a Thousand Columns, 30, 31 (photo)
Cuna tribe, 41 (photo), 43
Cuzco, 55–56

F
Feathers
  Maya and, 28
  trade of, 11

G
Goodyear, Charles, 49
Guaymi tribe, 43

I
Inca, 54–57
  in colonial times, 58
  trails of, 52 (photo)
Itzcoatl, 20

J
Jewelry, 11

K

Kaipo tribe, 50 (photo)
Kukulcan, 30. *See also* Quetzalcoatl.

L

Llamas, 57

M

Machu Picchu, 56 (photo)
Maize, 8, 9, 19, 27
Manco Capac, 54–55
Maya, 5, 9, 16, 26 (photo), 27, 28–31
  at present, 33
  Spanish invasion of, 32–33
Merchants, Aztec, 20, 22
Missionaries, 6 (photo), 11
Moche tribe, 53–54
Molas, 43
Muisca tribe, 40

O

Ocampo, Gonzalo de, 39
Ojeda, Alonso de, 39
Olmec tribe, 12 (photo), 13–15
Opata tribe, 9, 11

P

Palenque, 29 (photo)
Parrots, 11
Petén, 28–30
Pima tribe, 9, 11
Pizarro, Francisco, 58
Pochteca, 20, 22
Porters, Aztec, 20
Portobelo, 42 (photo), 43
Pottery
  Arawak, 36
  Olmec, 14

Q

Quetzalcoatl, 17
  Maya and, 30
  temple of, 17 (photo)

R

Rubber, 16, 49
Runners, Incan, 56

S

Salt, 31, 40
Seri tribe, 9–10
Slash-and-burn agriculture, 46
Sousa, Martin de, 48
Statues, Olmec, 13–14
Storehouses, Incan, 55, 57

T

Taino tribe, 34 (photo), 36, 38
Tenochtitlán, 19, 20, 21, 22–23, 25
Teotihuacán, 15–16
Tepexi, 21
Tikal, 29
Tlatelolco, 19
Toltec tribe, 17–18
Totonac tribe, 15–16, 24–25
Tula, 17–18
Tupa Inca, 55
Tupi tribe, 48, 49
Turquoise, 10

V

Vulcanization, 49

W

Waorani tribe, 50–51
Were-jaguars, 12 (photo)

Y

Yacatecuatli, 22
Yáñez Pinzón, Vicente, 48
Yanomami tribe, 44 (photo), 47 (photo), 50, 51
Yaqui tribe, 9, 11

Z

Zapotec tribe, 14 (photo)

Photo Credits

Cover and pages 6, 17, 32, 33, 42, 53, 56: ©Robert Frerck/Odyssey Productions/Chicago; pp. 9, 37: ©North Wind Picture Archives; p. 10: ©Robert B. Pickering; pp. 12, 14: ©Werner Forman Archive/Art Resource, NY; pp. 16, 21, 24, 26, 29, 31, 50: ©DDB Stock Photo; p. 34: ©Suzanne Murphy-Larronde/DDB Stock Photo; pp. 36, 41: ©Suzanne L. Murphy/DDB Stock Photo; pp. 44, 47: ©Victor Englebert/Photo Researchers; p. 46: ©Robert Fried/DDB Stock Photo; p. 52: ©Craig Duncan/DDB Stock Photo; p. 58: Jian Chen/Art Resource, NY.

NOV 1995

J 970.3 LUC
Lucas, Eileen.

Trade.

Rourke, c1995.

GLEN ROCK PUBLIC LIBRARY, NJ

3 9110 05024050 8

F
Y
12/95

Glen Rock Public Library
315 Rock Road
Glen Rock, N.J. 07452

201-670-3970